The ANiMaL iN Me is very plain to see!

Written by **Laurie C. Tye**   Photography by **THomaS D. MaNGeLSeN**

WHeN I aM HUNGRY,

I am like a great grizzly bear
with my mouth wide open.

WHEN I AM
SCARED,

I am like a white-tailed deer who is easily spooked.

WHeN I aM ANGRY,

I am like a ferocious lion protecting his pride.

WHeN I aM CURIOUS,

I am like a spotted owl scanning the forest floor checking things out.

WHEN I AM SAD,

I am like a dark brown bison standing alone in a white storm.

WHEN I FEEL LIKE SCREAMING,

I am like a coyote howling under a full moon.

WHeN I am LAZY,

I am like a harbor seal gazing into the bright blue sky.

WHEN I AM EXCITED,

I am like a little hummingbird constantly fluttering about.

WHeN I aM GRACEFUL,

I am like a beautiful swan with my wings wide open.

WHEN I AM
FAST,

I am like a cheetah
chasing a gazelle.

WHEN I AM TIRED,

I am like a Bengal tiger basking in the morning sunlight.

WHEN I AM HAVING FUN,

I am like a polar bear playing with my best friend.

WHEN I FEEL LOVED,

I am like a mountain lion cub snuggled in my mom's arms...

Because She
LOVES

ME more than any animal
in the whole world.

Goodnight Animals . . .

I am going to bed.

For Teea, Braden, Janessa, Lauren and Dallen for inspiring me
and allowing me to be creative. I love you. — LT

For my Aunt Helen Grennan, who has inspired my love of animals. — TM

Publisher: Laurie C. Tye
writeon3@live.com

Design by: Bud Spencer

Production Location: PRC Book Printing , Guangzhou, China
Date of Production: September 2015
Cohort: Batch 1
Website Info: www.pearlriverchinaprinting.com